THERE ONCE WAS A COWPOKE WHO SWALLOWED AN ANT

HELEN KETTEMAN

Illustrated by WILL TERRY

ALBERT WHITMAN & COMPANY
CHICAGO, ILLINOIS

There once was a cowpoke who swallowed an ant—
a fiery thing with a Texas-sized sting.

The cowpoke panted, and his voice got higher.

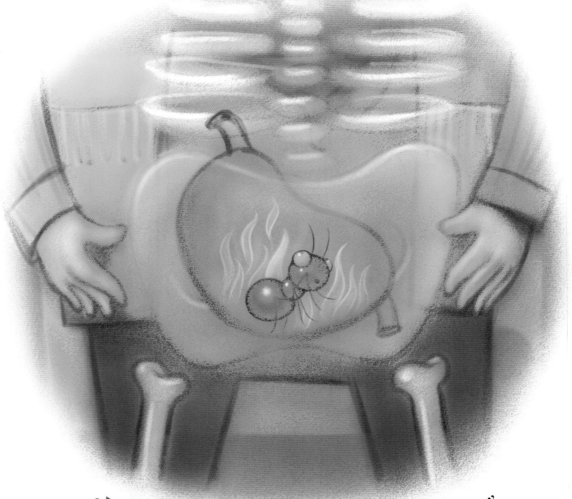

"**Yippie-ti-yay!** My stomach's on fire!"

So he swallowed a spider, leggy and hairy,
That was big as a bat and horribly scary.

He swallowed the spider
to bite the ant
that was stinging his stomach and making him pant.

But Spider's legs **wiggled** and **waggled**, and the cowpoke's stomach **jiggled** and **jaggled**.

So he swallowed a roadrunner, hungry and lean,
to dash right in and clean up the scene.

He swallowed Roadrunner
to eat the spider
to bite the ant
that was stinging his stomach
and making him pant.

But Roadrunner ran so lightning quick
that Cowpoke started to get seasick.

So he swallowed a lizard, a horned, spiky critter
that was scratchy to swallow and terribly bitter.

He swallowed the lizard
to chase Roadrunner
to eat the spider
to bite the ant

that was stinging his stomach
and making him pant.

But Lizard's skin was **scratchity-scritchy**
and the cowpoke's stomach got terribly itchy.

So he swallowed a 'dillo, the nine-banded type,
that was hard as a rock and smelled really ripe.

He swallowed the 'dillo

to scare the lizard

to chase Roadrunner

to eat the spider

to bite the ant

that was stinging his stomach

and making him pant.

But 'dillo's claws were sharp as a pointy old rake,

so the cowpoke rustled a rattle-tailed snake.

Then he swallowed that snake
to catch the 'dillo
to scare the lizard
to chase Roadrunner
to eat the spider
to bite the ant
that was stinging his stomach
and making him pant.

But Snake made his rattles shiver and shake
and the cowpoke's whole body quivered and quaked.

So he swallowed a boar, nasty and mean,
with the sharpest tusks he'd ever seen

But Boar's tusks jabbed the cowpoke instead,
and the cowpoke shouted, "I wish I wuz dead!"

He swallowed the boar
to poke the snake
to catch the 'dillo
to scare the lizard
to chase Roadrunner
to eat the spider
to bite the ant
that was stinging his stomach
and making him pant.

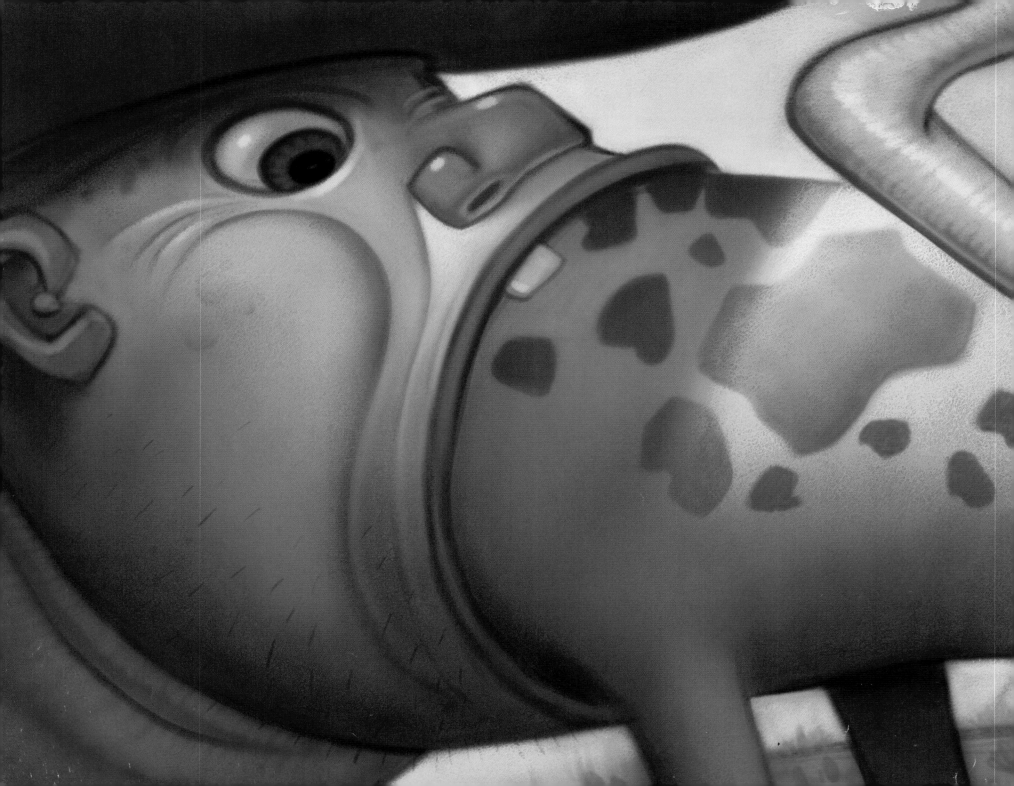

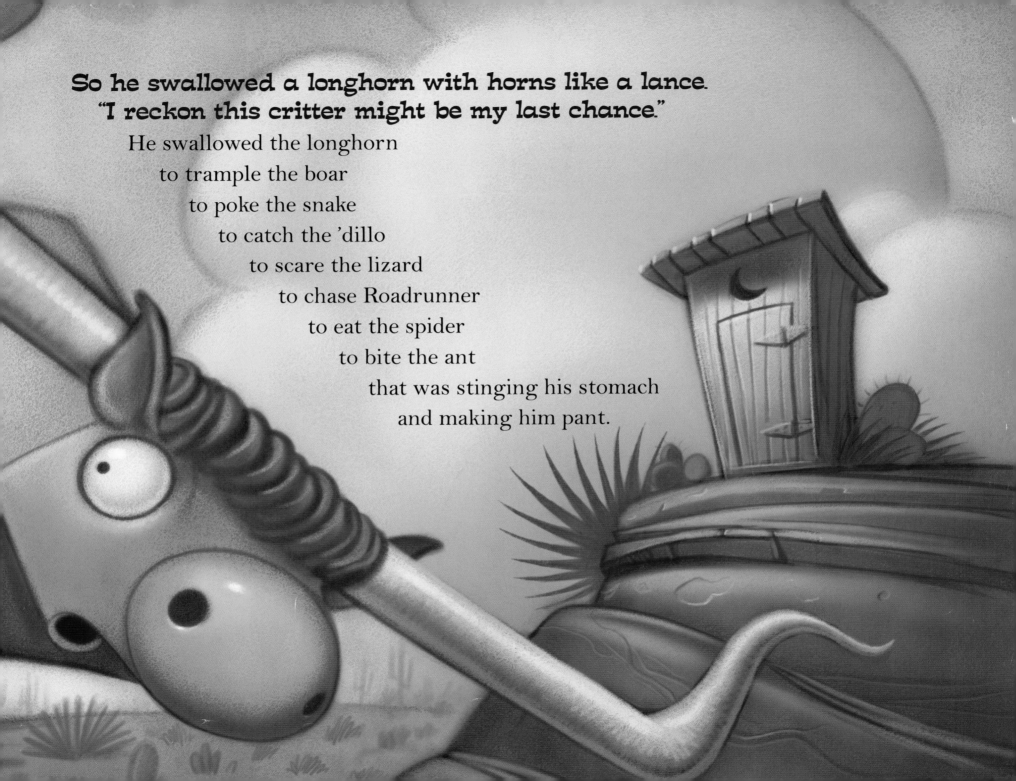

So he swallowed a longhorn with horns like a lance.
"I reckon this critter might be my last chance."
He swallowed the longhorn
to trample the boar
to poke the snake
to catch the 'dillo
to scare the lizard
to chase Roadrunner
to eat the spider
to bite the ant
that was stinging his stomach
and making him pant.

When Longhorn showed up, Boar set off like a flash.

Longhorn couldn't catch him to turn him to mash.

The cowpoke got mad and stomped on his hat.

"I'll just do it myself! I reckon that's that."

Then he saddled his horse, took his rope off the shelf.

"If I want it done right, I'll do it myself."

So he swallowed his rope,
he swallowed his horse,
and then he swallowed
himself, of course.

He swallowed himself
to lasso the longhorn
to trample the boar
to poke the snake
to catch the 'dillo
to scare the lizard
to chase Roadrunner
to eat the spider
to bite the ant
that was stinging his stomach
and making him pant.

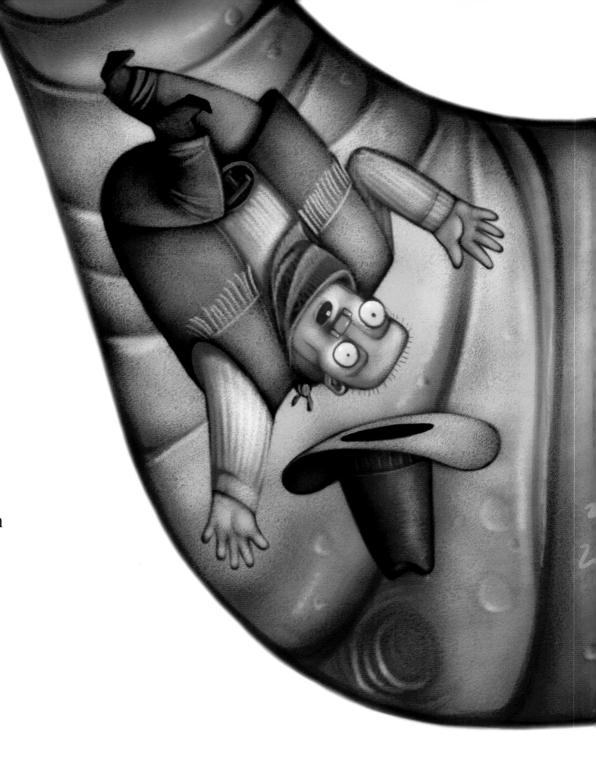

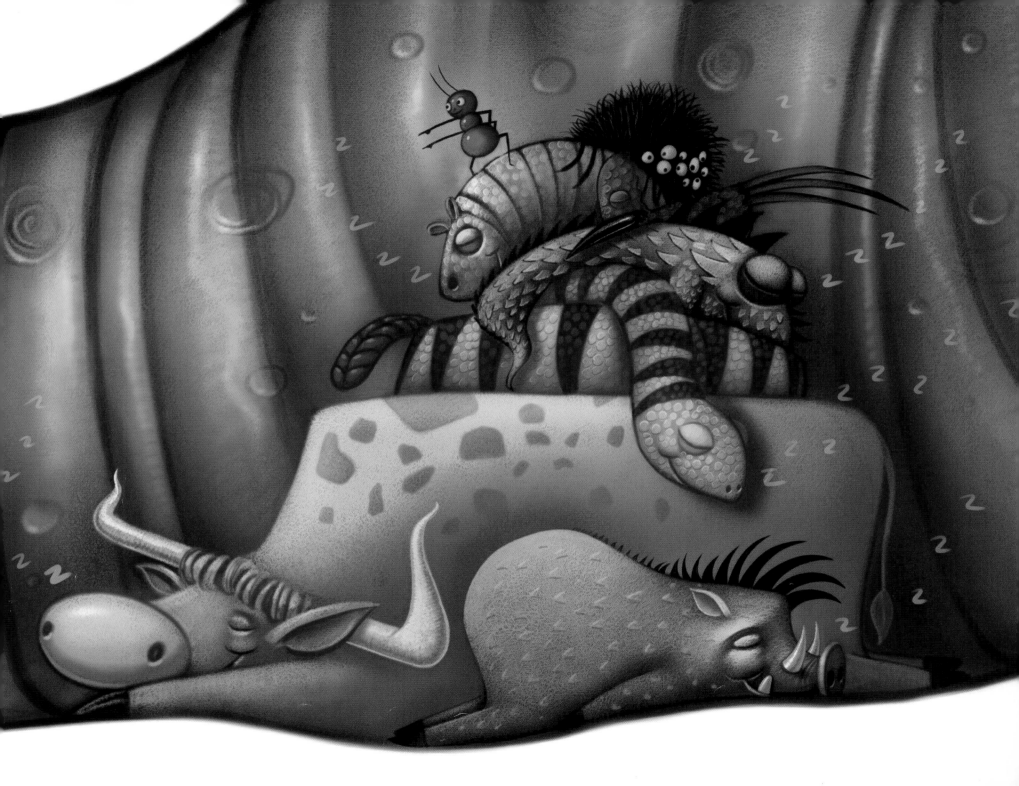

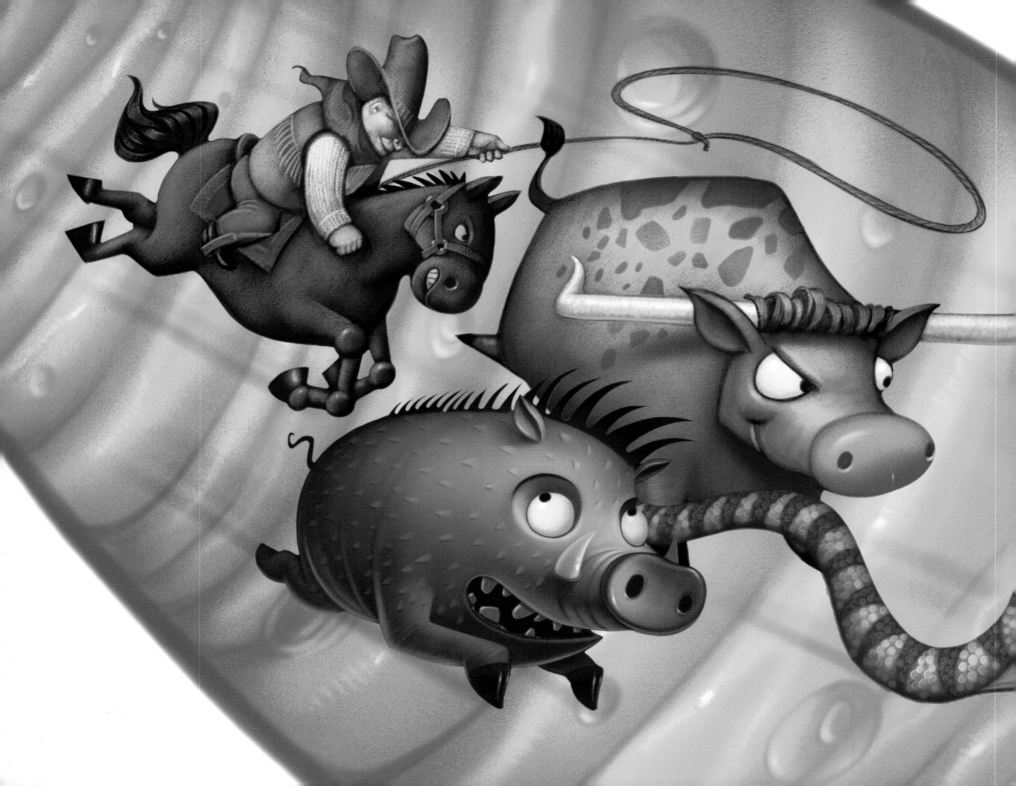

He jumped on his horse
and rode with great speed
and lassoed the longhorn
to start the stampede.

AND FINALLY...

OUT raced Longhorn
with the lasso a-flappin',

OUT followed Boar, his
hooves just a-tappin',

OUT slithered Snake,
in a very fast crawl,

OUT came the 'dillo
rolled in a ball.

OUT skittered Lizard,
hot on his trail,

OUT followed Roadrunner,
nippin' his tail…

OUT raced Spider,
jack-rabbit fast.

And then came the ant,
rid of **AT LAST**.

The cowpoke climbed off his horse.
"Whew! I'm all spent.
My get up and go has got up and went."

So he pulled his boots off his feet
and his hat off his head.

Then he shuffled inside and fell into bed.

For the Freeman family—Devin, Meghan, Shannon, Kate, and Lucy.
"No one fights alone." —HK

For Ray —WT

Library of Congress Cataloging-in-Publication Data

Ketteman, Helen.
There once was a cowpoke who swallowed an ant / by Helen Ketteman ;
illustrated by Will Terry.
pages cm
Summary: An illustrated version of the cumulative folk song in which the solution proves
worse that the predicament when a cowpoke swallows an ant with a sting the size of Texas.
ISBN 978-0-8075-7850-6 (hardcover)
1. Folk songs, English—England—Texts. [1. Folk songs—England.
2. Cowboys—Songs and music. 3. Humorous songs. 4. Songs.]
I. Terry, Will, 1966- illustrator. II. Little old lady who swallowed a fly. III. Title.
PZ8.3.K46The 2014
782.42—dc23
[E] 2013027328

The design is by Nick Tiemersma.

For more information about Albert Whitman & Company,
visit our web site at www.albertwhitman.com.